My r Book

by Jane Belk Moncure

illustrated by Linda Hohag

THE CHILD'S WORLD

ELGIN, ILLINOIS 60120

S0-AXT-172

1990 EDITION

Library of Congress Cataloging in Publication Data

Moncure, Jane Belk.
  My "r" book.

  (My first steps to reading)
  Rev. ed. of: My r sound box. © 1978.
  Summary: Little r finds a variety of animals and
things beginning with the letter r to put in his box.
  1. Children's stories, American.   [1. Alphabet]
I. Hohag, Linda. ill.   II. Moncure, Jane Belk.   My
r sound box.   III. Title.   IV. Series: Moncure,
Jane Belk.   My first steps to reading.
PZ7.M739Myr   1984   [E]   84-17555
ISBN 0-89565-290-0

Distributed by Childrens Press, 5440 North Cumberland Avenue,
Chicago, Illinois 60656

© 1984 The Child's World, Inc.
All rights reserved. Printed in U.S.A.
Special Revised Edition.

My "r" Book

(Blends are included in this book.)

Little  had a box.

"I will fill my box," he said.

Little  found rabbits

and radishes.

He put them into his box.

Little r found a rooster.

"In you go, rooster," he said.

box

He found a raccoon.

The raccoon ran.

Little r ran after him and...

put him into
the box.

Then he saw a rat.

The rat ran

Little  caught the rat.

Guess
where he put the rat?
Then he ran down the road.

box

Little  found a reindeer

and a rowboat.

He put all his things into
the rowboat.

Away he went.

It began to rain.

So he put on his raincoat.

Then he found a rhinoceros

and a raft.

So he put all his things

on the raft.

But the raft ran into a rock.

The reindeer fell off the raft.

Little found a rope.

He pulled the reindeer
back onto the raft.

"Let's rest," he said.

They rested under a rainbow.

Then the rabbits said,

"Let's run a race."

They ran up the road to...

a rose bush.

Little 🧒 said,

"Let's play
'Ring-Around
the-Roses'."

And they did.